Mystery Mob
and the
Time Machine

Roger Hurn

To re

Illustrated by
Stik

PISING STARS

Rising Stars UK Ltd.
22 Grafton Street, London W1S 4EX
www.risingstars-uk.com

The right of Roger Hurn to be identified as the author of this work
has been asserted by him in accordance with the Copyright,
Design and Patents Act 1988.

Published 2007
Reprinted 2008

Text, design and layout © Rising Stars UK Ltd.

Cover design: Button plc
Illustrator: Stik, Bill Greenhead for Illustration
Text design and typesetting: Andy Wilson
Publisher: Gill Budgell
Publishing manager: Sasha Morton
Editor: Catherine Baker
Series consultant: Cliff Moon

British Library Cataloguing in Publication Data.
A CIP record for this book is available from the British Library

ISBN: 978-1-84680-220-1

Printed in the UK by CPI Bookmarque, Croydon, CR0 4TD

Mixed Sources
Product group from well-managed
forests and other controlled sources
www.fsc.org Cert no. TT-COC-002227
© 1996 Forest Stewardship Council

Contents

Meet the Mystery Mob

Name:

Gummy

FYI: Gummy hasn't got much brain – and even fewer teeth.

Loves: Soup.

Hates: Toffee chews.

Fact: The brightest thing about him is his shirt.

Name:

Lee

FYI: If Lee was any cooler he'd be a cucumber.

Loves: Hip-hop.

Hates: Hopscotch.

Fact: He has his own designer label (which he peeled off a tin).

Name:

FYI: Rob lives in his own world – he's just visiting planet Earth.

Loves: Daydreaming.

Hates: Nightmares.

Fact: Rob always does his homework – he just forgets to write it down.

Name:

Dwayne

FYI: Dwayne is smarter than a tree full of owls.

Loves: Anything complicated.

Hates: Join-the-dots books.

Fact: If he was any brighter you could use him as a floodlight at football matches.

Name:

Chet

FYI: Chet is as brave as a lion with steel jaws.

Loves: Having adventures.

Hates: Knitting.

Fact: He's as tough as the chicken his granny cooks for his tea.

Name:

Adi

FYI: Adi is as happy as a football fan with tickets to the big match.

Loves: Telling jokes.

Hates: Moaning minnies.

Fact: He knows more jokes than a jumbo joke book.

About Time

It's Saturday and the Mystery Mob
are visiting Dwayne's uncle.
He's an inventor, and he's showing them
his latest invention – a time machine!

Adi   Billy Tibbs the school bully
             knows all about time travel.

Mystery Mob

             Does he?

Adi   Yes, he says if I don't stop
             telling silly jokes he'll knock me
             into the middle of next week!

Chet   I don't want to go into the future.
             I want to travel back in time.
             I want to see the dinosaurs.

Rob   I want to go back to lunchtime.

Lee   Why's that?

Rob   Because I'm still hungry.

Dwayne Shut up, you lot – I want
to try out the time machine.

Lee   Yeah! Me too! It's awesome.

Mystery Mob

Totally!

Dwayne's uncle

I'm sorry, guys – there's no way
I can let you use this machine.

Dwayne Oh! Why not?

Dwayne's uncle

It's way too risky for kids.
Only grown-up scientists like me
can be time travellers.

Dwayne But ...

Dwayne's uncle

But never mind, guys –
take a look at these jet-powered
football boots I've just made!

Lee They are soooo cool.

Chet Let's try them out.

Rob We can have a game
in the back garden.

Adi Come on – let's get going!

② Past Time

Chet, Adi, Rob and Lee go off
with Dwayne's uncle. Dwayne
and Gummy stay by the time machine.

Dwayne I'm not playing football.
I'm going in the time machine.

Gummy You can't. Your uncle said no.

Dwayne He didn't. He said we mustn't
use it. But all I want to do
is sit in it.

Gummy Well, I guess that's OK.

Dwayne Of course it is. Are you coming?

Gummy You bet I am.

The two boys climb inside
the time machine.

Gummy Look at all these buttons
and lights. This is great!

Dwayne It is, but don't touch anything.

Gummy I won't. Hey, what do you think
this big red button is for?

Dwayne I don't know.

Gummy There's only one way to find out.

Gummy puts his finger
on the big red button.

Dwayne (shouting) Don't press
that button!

Dwayne is too late. Gummy is already
pressing the button.

Gummy Oops! Sorry, I didn't mean to do that.

Dwayne You twit! Look what you've done. The hands on the clock are going backwards.

Gummy Are we going back in time?

Dwayne Yes, but where will we end up?

Gummy   Oh, that's easy.
We'll end up in the past.

Dwayne   Gummy, does your one brain cell
ever get lonely?

Gummy   No. It's got me to talk to.

Dwayne   Hey, the hands on the clock
have stopped.
I think we've arrived.

Gummy   So let's go and see where we are.

③ Time Out

Dwayne and Gummy step out
of the time machine. They are on a hill,
and they can see a big cave nearby.

A man dressed in clothes made of
animal skins is watching them.
He's got a stone axe in his hand.

Gummy   We've landed back
in the Stone Age.
Let's hope that caveman
is friendly.

Dwayne   I don't think he's pleased
to see us.

Gummy   Why not?

Dwayne   Well, for a start
he's jumping up and down
and shouting.

Gummy   And he's waving his axe at us.

Dwayne   That's never a good sign.

Gummy Why don't we go and talk to him
and try and calm him down?

Dwayne We don't speak Stone Age lingo.
And I don't want him to hit me
on the head with his axe.

Gummy Good point.

The caveman isn't cross.
He's seen something the boys
haven't seen. A huge sabre-toothed tiger
is creeping up behind them.

It stops. Then it opens its jaws and growls.

Dwayne Did you hear that growl?

Gummy Yes, I did. Hey, do you think
the caveman is trying to warn us
that a wild animal is close by?

Dwayne Oh yes. And it's
a sabre-toothed tiger.

Gummy How do you know?
You don't speak his lingo.

Dwayne I know because I'm looking at it.

Gummy (gulping) Yikes!
What are we going to do?

Dwayne Run for our lives!

The boys dash up to the caveman,
and he runs into the cave.
Dwayne and Gummy race after him.

The tiger prowls outside.
It won't go away.

It has them trapped.

④

A Hot Time

Dwayne How are we going to get rid
of that tiger?

Gummy I don't know. Maybe the caveman
will fight it with his stone axe.

Dwayne No he won't. Look at him!
He's as scared as we are.

The caveman is sitting in a corner
of the cave. He is shaking like a leaf.

Gummy So that's it. I'm going
to end up as cat food.

Dwayne It's not all bad.
At least you'll give the tiger
belly ache.

Gummy Very funny – I don't think.

Dwayne No, but I do – and I think
I've got an idea of how to save us.

Gummy What is it?

Dwayne Big cats are afraid of fire.
So if we set fire to a stick,
we can use it to scare off the tiger.

Gummy But cavemen don't have matches.

Dwayne No problem. I can start a fire
by rubbing two sticks together.

Gummy How does that work?

Dwayne Well, first I need some tinder.

Gummy What's tinder?

Dwayne Stuff that will burn.
Dry grass will do the trick.
Let's see if we can find some
in the cave.

The caveman's bed is a pile
of dried grass. The boys take some.
Then Dwayne picks up a thin stick
and a thicker stick from the floor
of the cave.

Dwayne These sticks will do nicely.

Gummy OK, so we've got dry grass
and two sticks. Now what?

Dwayne I put the thin stick on top
of the thick stick. Now I spin
the thin stick between the palms
of my hands – like so.

Gummy Cool.

Dwayne No – hot, actually.
The wood is starting to smoke.
Quick, let's put the hot wood
on to the dry grass.

Gummy Magic! The grass is on fire!

Dwayne You bet! Now let's put some sticks
on it and make a bonfire.

The boys soon have a fire blazing.

The caveman is amazed.
He has never seen fire before.
He thinks the boys are wizards.

Home Time

Gummy Let's grab a bunch
of burning sticks and go
and scare that old tiger away.

Dwayne Okay, but we'd better take care.
We don't want to get burnt.

Gummy Or eaten.

The boys jump out of the cave,
and wave the burning sticks at the tiger.

The flames scare the tiger. A spark
from one of the sticks lands on its tail.

Dwayne Uh-oh. We've set the tiger's tail
on fire.

Gummy That's done it. We've made it
mad. It'll eat us now for sure.

But the tiger gives a yelp and runs off.
It dives into a nearby river
and swims away.

Dwayne Wow – that was a close call.

Gummy I really hope we didn't hurt the tiger.

Dwayne We didn't. We just made things a bit hot for it, that's all.

Gummy Hey, look. The caveman
is using our sticks to make
his own fire. He's a copycat.

Dwayne Hmmm. I think we must be
the first people in history
to make fire.

Gummy   So will we be famous?

Dwayne   Let's hope not – we're not even supposed to be here. Hmmm … do you know what time it is?

Gummy   Stone Age time?

Dwayne   No, it's time to go home. And we need to get there before my uncle misses his time machine.

The two boys wave goodbye
to the caveman and jump back
into the time machine.

Gummy presses a big blue button.
The hands on the clock spin forward.

The boys get back home
in the nick of time. In fact,
it's just one second after they left.

Dwayne This is great!

Gummy How come?

Dwayne It means we get to play football
with the jet-powered boots
after all!

Gummy Hey, I love this time travel stuff.
But now it's time to go!
Race you out there!

About the author

Roger Hurn has:

- been an actor in 'The Exploding Trouser Company'
- played bass guitar in a rock band
- been given the title Malam Oga (wise teacher, big boss!) while on a storytelling trip to Africa.

Now he's a writer, and he hopes you like reading about the Mystery Mob as much as he likes writing about them.

The time travel quiz

Questions

1 Which TV doctor can travel in time?

2 Can you name a famous time machine?

3 Why didn't cavemen fight dinosaurs?

4 How did people tell the time before watches were invented?

5 Why couldn't you go to the dentist if you travelled back to King Henry the Eighth's time?

6 Why should you take an umbrella if you travelled back in time to a medieval town?

7 Why is it a good idea to take a packed lunch if you travel back in time to the Stone Age?

8 Why would you need to wear a clothes peg on your nose if you travelled back in time to Queen Victoria's London in the year 1858?

Answers

1 Doctor Who.
2 The Tardis.
3 The answer is not because they'd lose, it's because dinosaurs were extinct long before people came along.
4 They used sundials – though nobody wore them on their wrists!
5 Because there weren't any. Barbers pulled out your teeth – which was bad if you only wanted a haircut.
6 Because people didn't have indoor loos. Instead, they used potties at night – and they emptied their potties out of the bedroom window into the street below!
7 Because, until cave people discovered how to cook with fire, they ate raw meat and fish.
8 Because all the drains and cesspits overflowed into the River Thames. People called it 'The Great Stink'.

How did you score?

- If you got all eight answers correct, then you are really going places!

- If you got six answers correct, then you're ready to be Doctor Who's next assistant.

- If you got fewer than four answers correct, then the only time you'll be seeing a time lord is at teatime on the telly!

When I was a kid

Question Did you ever travel back in time when you were a kid?

Roger Yes. I went back to the Dark Ages.

Question What did you see there?

Roger Nothing – it was too dark.

Question Why is that time in history called the Dark Ages?

Roger Because there were so many knights.

Question OK, so you didn't really travel back in time – but were you any good at history when you were at school?

Roger No, I was hopeless.

Question Why was that?

Roger Because the teacher kept asking me questions about things that happened before I was born!

Adi's favourite time travel joke

When a knight in armour was killed in battle, what did they put on his gravestone?

Rust in peace!

How to be a time traveller

 Watch lots of old Doctor Who DVDs.

 Get a beautiful and clever person to be your assistant. If you can't find one, don't worry – the family dog will do. At least it won't think you're barking mad.

 Decide which time you want to travel to. Any time before 1870 is good – kids didn't have to go to school in those days.

 Make a time machine using your mum's digital alarm clock, the engine from your dad's lawn mower, and your sister's computer.

 Find out how one hour can last as long as a week, when they ground you for using their stuff!

Five fantastic facts about time

1 Long ago, people used to tell the time by looking at the Sun as it crossed the sky.
This didn't work if it was a rainy day.

2 The oldest type of clock is a sundial clock. They were invented about 5500 years ago.

3 The Ancient Egyptians invented water clocks. Water clocks were better than sundials. They could tell the time at night as well as during the day. The person who thought up that idea was no drip!

4 Time is different at different places. When it's early morning in Japan, it's late afternoon in New York.

5 One of the first alarm clocks worked by yanking a string that you tied to your little toe. Let's hope it didn't pull you right out of bed!

Time lingo

It'll only take a second What your mum says when she wants you to do a really boring job – like tidying up your bedroom.

I'll do it in a minute What you say when told to do a really boring job – like tidying up your bedroom.

Once in a blue moon Something that only happens very rarely – like you actually tidying up your bedroom.

There's plenty of time What your dad says when he's driving to the airport and your mum says you're going to miss the plane.

It's never too late
But it usually is –
especially when you're
trying to catch a plane.

Tempus fugit This is a Latin phrase meaning 'Time flies'. Hmmm … wonder which airline it uses?

Mystery Mob

Mystery Mob Set 1:

Mystery Mob and the Abominable Snowman
Mystery Mob and the Big Match
Mystery Mob and the Circus of Doom
Mystery Mob and the Creepy Castle
Mystery Mob and the Haunted Attic
Mystery Mob and the Hidden Treasure
Mystery Mob and the Magic Bottle
Mystery Mob and the Missing Millions
Mystery Mob and the Monster on the Moor
Mystery Mob and the Mummy's Curse
Mystery Mob and the Time Machine
Mystery Mob and the UFO

Mystery Mob Set 2:

Mystery Mob and the Ghost Town
Mystery Mob and the Bonfire Night Plot
Mystery Mob and the April Fools' Day Joker
Mystery Mob and the Great Pancake Race
Mystery Mob and the Scary Santa
Mystery Mob and the Conker Conspiracy
Mystery Mob and the Top Talent Contest
Mystery Mob and Midnight at the Waxworks
Mystery Mob and the Runaway Train
Mystery Mob and the Wrong Robot
Mystery Mob and the Day of the Dinosaurs
Mystery Mob and the Man Eating Tiger

RISING★STARS

Mystery Mob books are available from most booksellers.

**For mail order information
please call Rising Stars on 0871 47 23 010
or visit www.risingstars-uk.com**